P9-CCD-846

WELCOME TO
PASSPORT TO READING
A beginning reader's ticket to a brand-new world!

Every book in this program is designed to build read-along and read-alone skills, level by level, through engaging and enriching stories. As the reader turns each page, he or she will become more confident with new vocabulary, sight words, and comprehension.

These PASSPORT TO READING levels will help you choose the perfect book for every reader.

READING TOGETHER
Read short words in simple sentence structures together to begin a reader's journey.

READING OUT LOUD
Encourage developing readers to sound out words in more complex stories with simple vocabulary.

READING INDEPENDENTLY
Newly independent readers gain confidence reading more complex sentences with higher word counts.

READY TO READ MORE
Readers prepare for chapter books with fewer illustrations and longer paragraphs.

This book features sight words from the educator-supported Dolch Sight Words List. This encourages the reader to recognize commonly used vocabulary words, increasing reading speed and fluency.

For more information, please visit passporttoreadingbooks.com.

Enjoy the journey!

Copyright © 2016 Mattel, Inc. All rights reserved. EVER AFTER HIGH and associated trademarks are owned by and used under license from Mattel, Inc.

Cover design by Véronique Lefèvre Sweet/Carolyn Bull

In accordance with the U.S. Copyright Act of 1976, the scanning, uploading, and electronic sharing of any part of this book without the permission of the publisher is unlawful piracy and theft of the author's intellectual property. If you would like to use material from the book (other than for review purposes), prior written permission must be obtained by contacting the publisher at permissions@hbgusa.com. Thank you for your support of the author's rights.

Little, Brown and Company

Hachette Book Group
1290 Avenue of the Americas, New York, NY 10104
Visit us at lb-kids.com

Little, Brown and Company is a division of Hachette Book Group, Inc.
The Little, Brown name and logo are trademarks of Hachette Book Group, Inc.

The publisher is not responsible for websites (or their content) that are not owned by the publisher.

First Edition: February 2016

Library of Congress Control Number: 2015953996

ISBN 978-0-316-30180-0

10 9 8 7 6 5 4 3 2 1

CW

Printed in the United States of America

Passport to Reading titles are leveled by independent reviewers applying the standards developed by Irene Fountas and Gay Su Pinnell in *Matching Books to Readers: Using Leveled Books in Guided Reading*, Heinemann, 1999.

Let the Dragon Games Begin!

Adapted by Margaret Green

Based on the screenplay by
Sherry Klein, Shadi Petosky, and Keith Wagner

LITTLE, BROWN AND COMPANY
New York   Boston

Once upon a time,
Ever After High was the home
of the two best dragon riders
in all the land:
the Evil Queen and Snow White.

Because of their destinies,
the two rivals were very competitive.
Dragon riding could be dangerous.
Soon, dragon riding was banned
at Ever After High.
For many years, the Dragon Center
sat empty and unused.

That all changed when the daughters
of Snow White and the Evil Queen
arrived at Ever After High.
Apple White and Raven Queen
were roommates—and, against the odds,
they became friends.

Their friendship was not always
perfect, though.
The Evil Queen tricked Apple into
freeing her from her mirror prison.
The queen wanted to convince Raven
to accept her evil destiny,
so she disguised herself
as a student at Ever After High.

Meanwhile, Raven's dragon, Nevermore, went missing, and Raven and her friends searched the old Dragon Center to find her.

Not only did they find Nevermore
but they also found Daring Charming's
favorite dragon, Legend,
who was laying eggs!
Soon the eggs began to hatch.

Everyone loved the baby dragons.
They were too little to ride,
but the students had fun training
and playing with their new pets.

Then Snow White came to the school
to announce that there would be
Dragon Games at Ever After High
once again!

Soon the Evil Queen decided
to reveal herself.
Instead of sending her back
to her mirror prison,
Snow White decided to let her stay
so they could coach
the new dragon-riding teams.

Raven refused to join a team.
So the Evil Queen chose Apple
as captain of the Dark Team.
Snow White asked Darling Charming
to be captain of the Light Team.

Snow White and the Evil Queen
showed off some of their
dragon-riding skills
on Legend and Nevermore.
They were spelltacular riders!

Then the new teams took to the field
with their dragons.
This was a little less exciting,
because these dragons could not
fly like the grown-up dragons could!

During a break, the girls took their dragons back to the stables to feed them.

They did not know that the Evil Queen had ordered Faybelle Thorn to put a growth formula in the dragon food.

The dragons began to grow
very quickly.
Soon they were big enough to ride!

"Remember, this is just a game!"
Snow White told the Light Team.
"This is not just a game!" the
Evil Queen shouted at her team.
"Victory is all that matters!"

Apple scored the first goal of the game.
Then, when Darling was about to score,
Apple flew at her and
knocked her off her dragon!

Now the Light Team did not
have enough players!
Snow White was about to forfeit
when Raven spoke up.
"Not so fast," she said.
Raven was going to play!

Up in the air, Raven confronted Apple.
"My mom is free and Darling is hurt!"
she cried.
"It was not supposed to be like this,"
Apple said. "But doesn't it make you angry?"
She wanted Raven to turn evil
and fulfill their destinies.

"I am not playing games
anymore," Raven declared.
She tossed the ball to Apple
and steered Nevermore
out of the arena.

Apple was frustrated,
but she still wanted to win the game.
She soared through the air,
gathering points as she went.
Then she hurled the ball
through the goal.

Raven was not going to turn
evil herself, so her mother
decided to make it seem like she was.
The Evil Queen cast a spell on
Nevermore to make her breathe
fire and destroy the castle.
Then the Evil Queen took control
of the school!

Luckily, Raven's friends knew
she was not really evil.
Darling helped her
come up with a plan to
take back Ever After High.

The riders took off on their dragons
to face the Evil Queen.

Just in time, Apple realized
that her friendship with Raven
was more important than
her Happily Ever After.
She rode with her friends,
carrying a special mirror that could
trap the Evil Queen once again.

Apple tried to pull the Evil Queen
into the mirror, but it did not work.
"The mirror is not strong enough
without you!" Apple cried to Raven.
When Raven added her powers to
the mirror's, the two friends were
able to defeat the Evil Queen.

The force of the Evil Queen
entering the mirror knocked
Apple and Raven off their dragons!
They fell toward the ground,
but Nevermore scooped them up
just in time.

Apple and Raven were back to
being best friends forever after.

Their adventure had one
very good result: Ever After High
was once again home to Dragon Games!
With the Evil Queen gone,
they really were all fun and games.

And even though she was trapped in her mirror, Raven's mother was still her number one fan.